H. G. WELLS

The Time Machine

Adapted by Les Martin

Illustrated by John Edens

HAMPTON-BROWN

THE EXCHANGE

What would
happen if we
could see the future?

The Time Machine by H. G. Wells, adapted by Les Martin, illustrated by John Edens.
Text copyright © 1990 by Random House, Inc. Illustrations copyright © 1990 by John Edens.
Cover illustration copyright © 1994 by Tom Newsom. Cover design by Fabia Wargin Design
and Creative Media Applications, Inc. Published by arrangement with Random House
Children's Books, a division of Random House, Inc. New York, New York, U.S.A.
All rights reserved.

On-Page Coach™ (introductions, questions, on-page glossaries),
The Exchange, back cover summary © Hampton-Brown.

Hampton-Brown
P.O. Box 223220
Carmel, California 93922
800-333-3510
www.hampton-brown.com

Printed in the United States of America

ISBN-13: 978-0-7362-2790-2
ISBN-10: 0-7362-2790-3

06 07 08 09 10 11 12 13 14 10 9 8 7 6 5 4 3 2

It is 1895. A man builds a machine. It can help him travel through time. He tells his friends about it. They don't think it will work.

Chapter One

Call me the Time Traveler. That is what my friends now call me. But even they do not completely believe my story. Will you? I wonder.

I can only write it all down. I can only hope that readers will **see** I tell the truth. Readers now or in the future. **Only time will tell.**

Time. That word brings me to the start of my story. The start of my journey. The most amazing journey anyone has ever taken.

First, a few words about myself. I am an inventor. A good one. My inventions have **won me fame and fortune**. But they were nothing compared with my latest, greatest one.

I began work on this new invention two years

....

see know

Only time will tell. Readers will only know the truth in the future.

won me fame and fortune made me famous and rich

ago. Two weeks ago I **could report success** at last.

I invited my four best friends to my house in London. The date was September 15, 1895.

My friends were educated men. A doctor. A writer. A politician. A psychologist. But they listened like schoolchildren as I explained my invention.

"There are three **dimensions** in our world," I said. "We can see them easily. Length. Height. Thickness. But there is another dimension we cannot see.

"Yet we know it is there. It is part of everything in the world. This other dimension is the Fourth Dimension. It is Time."

I **let my words sink in**. Then I went on. "We can move through the first three dimensions. We can go backward and forward. We can go right and left. Up and down. Then why can't we move through the Fourth Dimension, too? A train travels on land. A ship on water. A balloon in the air. So why not a machine through time?"

....

could report success was successful

dimensions ways to measure things

let my words sink in waited for them to understand what I said

I let my friends think about it. Then I gave them my news. "I want you to be the first to know. I have built just such a machine."

My friends' mouths dropped open. The writer was the first to speak.

"A Time Machine?" he said with a smile. "I never knew you had such a wild imagination. You should try writing fiction. You could create a new kind. Call it science-fiction."

The psychologist **chimed in**. "I know how you like to joke. Or else I'd tell you **to have your head examined**. By me, of course. For a fat fee."

The doctor took me more seriously. "You've been working too hard lately. Get out of your workshop for a while. A vacation would do you good. Perhaps a trip."

The politician just said, "**Pity** there isn't such a machine. I'd like a quick trip to the future. To see how the election next month turns out."

The writer **got into the spirit**. "I'd like a time trip, too. What a story I could write! Even better, a

....

chimed in agreed

to have your head examined that you are crazy

Pity It is too bad

got into the spirit wanted to tell his idea, too

book. My publishers would love it."

"I'd love to see the medical marvels, " the doctor said. His eyes were shining. "Think of it. A world where no one has to be sick."

"Or else a world in ruins," the politician said. He shook his head. "Weapons will be terrible. I wonder **if the future holds peace or war**? Freedom or slavery?"

"Bravo, my friend," the psychologist said to me. "You've dreamed up a great way to make dinner interesting. Talking about the future brings out all our hopes. And all our fears."

"Tell me, then, did I dream up this?" I asked. "Is this a dream?"

I took an object the size of a clock from the cabinet. I set it on the table.

My friends examined it. It had a metal frame. Inside the frame was an engine. It was made of **rare crystal**. **A pair of white ivory levers was** attached to the engine. In front of them was a tiny chair.

"It's made beautifully," the doctor said.

....

if the future holds peace or war if there will be peace or war in the future

rare crystal expensive glass that is hard to find

A pair of white ivory levers was Two handles were

"Made **by hand**," I said. "My hand."

"But what is it?" the writer asked.

"A better question is, what does it do," I said.

I pressed down on a lever.

At first the frame shook violently. Then the shaking stopped. The whole object became **fainter and fainter**. It was like a drawing in disappearing ink. Within two minutes it was gone. **No trace of it was left.**

The writer clapped his hands in loud applause. "I was wrong when I told you to write fiction," he said. "You should be a magician. That trick would make you a **fortune** on the stage."

"Yes, it is very clever indeed," the psychologist agreed. "How did you do it? With mirrors? And where have you hidden it?"

"Why, it's right where you saw it last," I said. I pointed to the tabletop. "But it is not here in the present. It is here in the future. One thousand years in the future."

"You mean—?" the politician began. Then he

....

by hand with a worker's hands and tools; without machines

fainter and fainter more difficult to see

No trace of it was left. The machine was gone.

fortune a lot of money

stopped and laughed. "**You almost had me fooled** for a moment. But you would never risk losing such a **precious object**. Not just to **show off** for a few friends."

I smiled. "Losing it doesn't matter to me now. It was only a model. A model I no longer need. For I have finished building the real thing."

....

You almost had me fooled I almost believed you
precious object valuable thing
show off make yourself look good

BEFORE YOU MOVE ON...

1. **Character's Point of View** The Time Traveler doesn't think his friends or the readers will believe his story. Why not?

2. **Summarize** Reread pages 8 and 9. What happened to the little time machine when the Time Traveler pressed the lever?

LOOK AHEAD Read pages 10–15 to find out about the Time Traveler's future dinner plans.

The Time Traveler experiments with the real time machine. He travels more than five hours in just two minutes.

Chapter Two

My friends **gathered** around the machine in my workshop. It was exactly like the model I had shown them. Only it was twenty times larger.

"You mean you sit in that chair? Pull that lever? And travel into the future?" the writer asked.

"Or into the past," I said. "Whichever I choose."

"And which would you choose?" the psychologist asked.

"The future first," I said. "It is **the unknown** that interests me the most."

"And do we get to see it **in action**?" the politician asked.

"Perhaps take a ride ourselves?" the doctor suggested.

....

gathered stood in a group

the unknown what I do not know

in action work

"Not yet," I answered. "I still have a few things to **tinker with**. Then it will be ready to go."

My friends smiled.

"You still don't believe me," I said. I pretended to be angry. "Very well, then. Come to dinner here a week from now. I promise to show you then that my Time Machine works."

After my friends left, it was my turn to smile. My friends had been right about one thing. I did like jokes.

I had told them I still had to tinker with my machine. But there was one thing I had not told them. The tinkering would take only a few hours. Then my Time Machine would be ready.

Before I started to work, I called in my housekeeper. I told her to cook dinner for my friends next week. The best dinner she could make. And I handed her a note. She was to give it to them when they arrived.

The note said I was sorry not to greet them. But it promised I would join them before the evening ended.

....

tinker with fix

Then I **set** to work. The work was very delicate. I had to make sure the size of the levers was just right. To the smallest fraction of an inch.

One lever **was to** start the machine traveling through time. Push it up, and it went into the past. Pull it down, and it went into the future. The other lever was to stop it wherever I wanted.

But I should not say "wherever." Rather, "whenever." Because I would be staying in the same **spot**. Only the time would be changed.

It was almost four in the morning. I had finished my work. I measured the levers one last time. Now only one thing was left to do. To give the Time Machine its first test.

I sat down in the seat of the Time Machine. I looked at my pocket watch. Nineteen after four. I held my breath as I gripped the lever. I pulled it down a tiny bit.

How can I say what it felt like? Only that it felt like falling. Falling through endless space.

....

set started

was to would

spot place

My stomach was trying to squeeze into my throat. My mouth was open. It looked like the mouth of a fish. A fish **gasping in air**.

Quickly I pulled the stop lever. There was a **slight** bump. The machine stopped.

I looked around me. **My heart sank.**

....

My stomach was trying to squeeze into my throat. I felt sick.

gasping in air trying to breathe

slight small

My heart sank. I felt very unhappy.

My tools were where I had laid them. My coat still hung over a chair. My workshop was just as I had left it. My machine was a failure.

Then I saw daylight in the window. My heart beat faster. I looked at a clock on the mantle. It said half past nine. I pulled out my pocket watch. **It read** twenty-one minutes after four.

I had traveled more than five hours in just two minutes. The Time Machine worked!

I suppose I should have stopped then. I should have **planned my next move**. But I had waited too long for this moment. I could not wait any longer to journey through time.

....

It read The time was
planned my next move thought about what to do next

BEFORE YOU MOVE ON...

1. **Inference** Reread page 12. Why do you think the Time Traveler will not be there to greet his friends when they come for dinner?

2. **Conclusions** How did the Time Traveler know his machine worked?

LOOK AHEAD Read pages 16–17 to find out how the Time Traveler decides to use his machine next.

I pulled down the lever again. This time I pulled it a bit harder. And farther. Time outside the machine speeded up.

I saw my housekeeper **whiz** into the room. She cleaned it **in record time**. She shot out the door. It was clear she could not see me.

I pulled the lever farther down. The window grew dark. Then it brightened. Then it darkened again. Days **went by** like blinking lights.

I pulled down on the lever still more. Daylight and darkness **became a blur**. The windows and walls of my workshop vanished.

The machine was swaying now. My mind was swaying, too, as if it were drunk. It *was* drunk. Drunk with power. I wanted to pull the lever all the way down. I did.

Around me was a world of wonders. Huge buildings rising taller and taller. Skies changing from dark gray to bright blue. A countryside that grew greener and greener.

What a fantastic show! It was hard to turn my eyes away. But at last I did.

....

whiz come quickly
in record time faster than ever
went by passed
became a blur were hard to see

I looked at the dials. They told me how fast and far I was traveling. I was shocked. I had gone much faster and farther than I thought.

I was in the year 802,701 A.D.

Those huge numbers made me **lose my head**. I was in a panic. I yanked hard on the stop lever.

I paid the price. The stop was too sharp. The machine tipped over. I was thrown from my seat.

Stunned, I lay on soft green grass. I heard a very loud thunderclap. **A shower of hailstones** stung my face. It was impossible to see.

"A fine welcome," I muttered. "A man travels over 800,000 years for a visit. And this is the greeting he gets!"

Then the hail thinned. The sun shone through a break in the clouds.

And I **got my first good look** at the world of the future.

I was in the year 802,701 A.D. I had traveled more than 800,000 years into the future.

lose my head very scared

A shower of hailstones Many small balls of ice

got my first good look looked closely for the first time

BEFORE YOU MOVE ON...

1. **Character's Motive** Why did the Time Traveler decide to pull the lever again?

2. **Cause and Effect** Reread page 17. What made the machine stop in the year 802,701 A.D.?

LOOK AHEAD Read pages 18–24 to find out what the Time Traveler sees when the hail clears.

The Time Traveler sees an old statue and new, huge buildings. He finds people, too. They are thin, gentle, and happy. They speak a different language.

Chapter Three

Through the thinning hail I saw a white shape. Then the hail stopped completely. **Blue spread over the sky.** And I was staring at a huge white marble statue. On a high base of bronze. A Sphinx. With the head of a woman. A lion's body. And an eagle's outspread wings. It **towered** above me.

So this was what the future world was like, I thought. The White Sphinx was the work of a great artist. Clearly **the future** loved beauty.

....

Blue spread over the sky. The sky was blue.

towered was very high

the future people in the future

But then I looked more closely. The bronze base **was green with mold**. The Sphinx's face was partly worn away.

Had civilization fallen apart? It did not seem so. In the distance I could see giant buildings. They made those of my time seem small and ugly.

I **stared hard** at those buildings. I saw tiny shapes on a terrace. They were living creatures. People! One was pointing at me.

....

was green with mold had green dirt on it
stared hard looked for a long time

Suddenly I felt afraid. What would these people think of me? Do to me? To them I was a **cave man**. Or even an animal. They might want to cage me. Or perhaps even kill me.

I tensed my muscles and pushed my Time Machine upright. I checked it over. Nothing was broken. I could relax. If I found myself in danger, I could escape.

I climbed into the Time Machine and sat down. I gripped the lever. Then I heard someone coming through the bushes nearby. **My grip tightened.** I was ready for the people of the future!

A man came out of the bushes. I let go of the lever. I could see no danger.

This man was no more than four feet tall. He was very **slender**. He wore a short purple robe with a thin belt. His legs were bare. Soft sandals were on his feet.

Everything about him was beautiful. But very delicate. Like a perfect flower that would die in a cold wind. But I could feel how warm the air was in this world.

....

cave man man from the past, who lived in a cave
My grip tightened. I held the lever more tightly.
slender thin

Others came behind him. Their clothes were
like his. But the colors all were different. The males
and females looked very much alike. I could hardly
tell them apart.

There was no fear on their lovely faces.
They crowded around me. They were smiling and
laughing. I smiled back. How foolish I had been to

....

There was no fear on their lovely faces. They did not
seem afraid.

worry. These people did not know the meaning of fear. They had no reason to hate or to harm.

I let them touch me with their soft hands. I let them touch my machine, too. They seemed to want to make sure we were real. Their voices were gentle and musical. They sounded like birds **cooing**, as they spoke. Their language was strange to me. **I could not understand a word.**

---

cooing making soft sounds

I could not understand a word. I could not understand anything they said.

BEFORE YOU MOVE ON...

1. **Summarize** Reread pages 19–21. What did the Time Traveler conclude from looking at the Sphinx and the buildings?

2. **Cause and Effect** Reread pages 22–24. What made the Time Traveler get into his machine?

LOOK AHEAD Read pages 25–29 to find out why no one talked to the Time Traveler.

Then something began to trouble me.

None of them showed any interest in talking to me. Nobody asked me questions. Nobody tried to find out who I was.

But perhaps they already knew. Yes, that was it! They already **had all the answers**.

Still, I had to make sure. I pointed to the sun. I wanted to **express the idea of time**.

My first visitor looked puzzled. Then he clapped his hands in delight. He made the sound of a thunderclap. The others joined in. They made the same sounds.

I was **astounded**. These people thought I had fallen from the sky. Fallen like the hail. They had the minds of five-year-olds.

I tried to **make sense of this**. I could not. Then the little people made eating motions with their hands. They patted their stomachs. And I suddenly realized how hungry I was. After all, I had not eaten in 800,000 years! I went with them to their dining hall.

But first I took care to remove the levers from

....

had all the answers knew everything about me

express the idea of time say that I came from a different time

astounded very surprised

make sense of this understand why the people acted this way

the Time Machine. I put them in my pocket to be safe. Some of these people might play with the machine while I was gone. They were **childlike enough** to do that.

We walked to the dining hall. Many of the great buildings we passed seemed empty. There were cracks in the windows. The colors of the tiles were faded. I remembered how worn the White Sphinx looked. It seemed that I had been right: This world was **going downhill**!

When we entered the dining hall, I began to see why.

The hall was huge. It had stained-glass windows and a stainless metal floor. There were panes missing from the windows. The floor was worn by many feet over many years.

The dining tables and chairs were polished stone. Many of the chairs were empty. There was much more food on the tables than we needed. Only a few hundred people were eating in the great dining hall.

I sat down and began eating. The food was very good. The fruits and vegetables on the table were

....

childlike enough like children so they might try
going downhill not as good as the past

strange to me. But I found they were delicious. I saw no meat. There were people of my own time who said that eating **flesh** was wrong. It seemed that **their point of view had won out**.

There were no plates or knives and forks. Everything was eaten by hand. Cleaning up was easy. Leftovers were thrown into holes in the floor. They disappeared below.

During the meal, I began to learn the language of the future. I pointed to different things. I asked people to say their names. **It was slow going.** People would come up to me. They would look at me. Then they would **drift off**. **I could only hold their interest** for a minute or two.

After eating, the people began singing and dancing. Nobody even glanced at me when I left the hall. I wanted to be alone. I had to put my thoughts together.

There was a full moon out. I strolled along. I saw flowers more beautiful than I had ever seen before.

....

flesh meat

their point of view had won out the people in the future thought that eating meat was wrong, too

It was slow going. It took a long time.

drift off go away

I could only hold their interest They would listen to me only

Fruits and vegetables grew wild everywhere. I saw no weeds. No insects. No animals. **No trace of any threat to an endless harvest of food.**

I thought of the people I had met. They showed no signs of sickness. Or injury. Or even age. They enjoyed perfect health. Perfect happiness. In a perfect world.

This then was the reason for the decay I had seen. The neglect of the buildings. The green mold on the Sphinx's base. People had lost the need to work to make life better. They had everything they wanted. They were happy . . . well, simply to be happy.

Could I blame them? I found it hard to. Yet at the same time I found it sad. This was what humans had become. **Creatures of pleasure.** They had no thoughts in their minds. Their lives were made up of eating, dancing, singing, playing.

By now I had reached the White Sphinx. I looked up at it and said, "Answer me this riddle, Sphinx. Is this what all of history has led to? All the work of all the scientists? And artists? And thinkers? And builders? Did they do so much to produce so little?

....

No trace of any threat to an endless harvest of food. There was nothing to kill the food that always grew.

Creatures of pleasure. People who had fun all the time.

Did all their efforts produce a world of people who are forever children?"

I received the only answer a Sphinx ever gives. Silence. I sighed in despair. I would have to take my unanswered question back to my own time.

Then all my thoughts were washed away. **A wave of horror hit me.** It was like the thunderclap that greeted me when I arrived.

I saw that my Time Machine was gone!

....

A wave of horror hit me.
I felt very scared.

BEFORE YOU MOVE ON...

1. **Conclusions** Reread page 25. What made the Time Traveler think the people were like children?

2. **Inference** Why was the Time Traveler disappointed in the future?

LOOK AHEAD Read pages 30–35 to find out if the Time Traveler finds his machine.

*The Time Traveler looks for his machine alone,
but he needs help. He needs to make friends with
someone from this future world.*

Chapter Four

I could not **believe my eyes**. Or rather I did not *want* to believe my eyes. The thought was too terrible.

I could not return to my own time. I was trapped in the future forever.

For a moment I froze. I was **in shock**. Then I forced myself to think. And move.

The Time Machine had to be here. The people must have hidden it nearby. They were too weak to move it far. Maybe **this was their idea of playing hide-and-seek**. They were childish enough.

Desperately I searched the bushes around the grass field. Branches scratched my face. Blood ran

....

believe my eyes understand what I saw

in shock too surprised to think or act

this was their idea of playing hide-and-seek they were playing a game

down my cheek. I hardly noticed. I still had not found my Time Machine.

Sweat soaked my shirt. My eyes burned with anger. **The game had gone far enough.** I ran back to the dining hall. It was empty.

Where had they gone? I went back out into the night. Another building was nearby. It was a palace fit for a king.

I found the door open. I was not surprised. I had not found a door locked yet. Inside, people were sleeping. There were more than twenty of them. They were lying on cushions on the marble floor.

"Wake up!" I shouted. **In my anger** I forgot that they did not know my language. "Where is my machine?"

They may not have understood my words. But the anger in my voice was clear. **That, and the fist I waved at them.**

I made myself even clearer. I pulled one of them to his feet. I shook him hard. Then I let him go. He stood trembling before me.

....

The game had gone far enough. I was not going to guess where the time machine was.

In my anger I was so angry that

That, and the fist I waved at them. I sounded angry, and I looked like I was ready to fight them.

By now they were all awake. A strange look came over their beautiful faces. I realized that look was new to them. Probably they did not even know what that look was. But I did.

It was fear.

I forgot my anger. I would not be the one who taught these people fear.

I would use a better method to find my Time Machine. I would learn their ways, their language. Then I could tell them how much I wanted the machine. Once they knew, they would give it back.

Besides, I told myself, I was in no hurry. I had traveled so far to find out what **the future held**. I could take a few days to find out more. I did not even have to worry about the dinner with my friends. I could come home a week after I had left. I was no longer **a slave of Time**. I was its master.

I patted the shaking man before me on the shoulder. It is the way one calms any scared creature. It worked. He smiled and yawned. Then he lay down to go back to sleep.

Then I lay down and went to sleep myself. Maybe in the morning my Time Machine would

....

the future held I would see in the future
a slave of Time someone who had to care about time

be back. Maybe the theft would turn out to be a bad dream.

It did not. But the next day it seemed less of a nightmare.

When I awoke, I went back to the White Sphinx. I was hunting for clues. A group of people followed me. They had already forgotten the fear I had caused. I was once again **an object of fun**. Like a new toy or game.

I reached the spot where my Time Machine had been. There I saw what I had not seen in my panic. In the soft grass were two tracks. They **marked** where my Time Machine had been dragged away. The tracks led straight to the bronze base of the White Sphinx.

....

an object of fun something for them to play with
marked showed

BEFORE YOU MOVE ON...

1. **Conclusions** On page 35, the Time Traveler found two tracks. What did they show?

2. **Character** At first the Time Traveler yelled at the people. Reread page 33 and tell how he changed.

LOOK AHEAD Read to page 39 to find out why the people won't help the Time Traveler get his machine.

I banged with my fist on the base. It was **hollow**.

Now I knew where my Time Machine was.
I looked more closely at the base. I saw almost invisible lines. They marked a sliding door. All I had to do was open that door. My Time Machine would be waiting.

But how to do it? There were no handles, knobs, or levers. I had to figure out how the door worked. Or else find tools to force it open.

I turned to ask for help. But the people who had followed me were gone. Then I saw one of them. He was watching me from the bushes. Before he could get away, I grabbed him. I dragged him to the bronze base. I tried to make him understand what I wanted. I shoved his face close to the secret door.

The look on his face stopped me. He looked sick. It was as if I were forcing something horrible down his throat. **His eyes begged me** to let him go. And I did. He ran away as fast as his legs would go.

I watched him leave. These children would not **be any help**. Then I looked around for something, anything, I could use. I picked up a rock and

....

hollow empty
His eyes begged me He had a look that showed he wanted me
be any help help me

banged on the door. It made a few dents. But that was all.

I would have to **go back to my first plan**. I would learn to talk to these people. I'd ask them to give back my Time Machine. Or else tell me how to get at it.

I gave the door one last bang. Then I tossed my rock away. It was useless.

Then I heard it. Or at least I thought I heard it.

A sound from behind the door. A sound like a **chuckle**.

It stopped. I pressed my ear against the bronze. But I heard nothing more.

I shrugged. Perhaps the sound had not come from behind the door. It could have been leaves on the trees. It did not matter. I could not worry about odd noises. I had more important things to do.

I soon had another **worry on my hands**. A much more serious one.

The people who had been so friendly before now stayed away from me. I could guess why. It had to

----

go back to my first plan try my first idea
chuckle laugh
worry on my hands problem

do with my trying to open the bronze door. I must have broken some kind of rule. I had somehow become **unclean**.

They **shrank from me when I tried to make contact**. My concern grew. How could I get them to give me what I needed so badly? The knowledge. And the tools.

Then an accident gave me what I needed most of all.

A friend.

....

unclean a bad person

shrank from me when I tried to make contact turned away when I went near them

BEFORE YOU MOVE ON...

1. **Sequence** The people were too scared of the Sphinx to help the Time Traveler. What did he do next?

2. **Conflict** Reread pages 38–39. Why did the Time Traveler feel the people were no longer friendly to him?

LOOK AHEAD Read pages 40–44 to meet the Time Traveler's new friend.

The Time Traveler meets Weena. He learns that there are creatures that live underground called Morlocks. Weena's people are called Eloi.

Chapter Five

I was walking in the bright morning sunlight. I saw that the weather in England **had changed for the better**. It was delightfully warm out. All around me people were enjoying themselves. They were playing tag and other simple games. They were dancing to songs that others sang. They were walking **hand in hand**.

It was a scene of perfect peace and happiness. But suddenly **it was shattered by a scream**.

The scream came from the river. A swimmer was crying for help.

Amazingly, no one seemed to come. The people around me kept on smiling, laughing, singing,

....

had changed for the better was better
hand in hand and holding each other's hands
it was shattered by a scream someone screamed

chattering. No one made a move to go to the rescue.

I had to act fast. The river current was carrying the swimmer away. I **stripped** off my clothes and dove in. I reached the swimmer just in time.

I saw the swimmer was a woman. I carried her to the shore. She was small and beautiful, like all her people. I lay her down on the grass. I rubbed her **chilled** arms and legs with my shirt. At last she stopped shivering.

That was how I met Weena. She taught me her name. Then she taught me her language. And she taught me something even more important. That people still knew how to be grateful.

I did not expect to see her again after she went off. These people could not **keep their minds on** anything. She would quickly forget how I saved her.

But that afternoon Weena joined me again. Smiling, she handed me a wreath of lovely flowers. Then she kissed my hands. After that, she refused to leave my side. She went everywhere I did.

I say this, even though she did not like certain

....

stripped took
chilled cold
keep their minds on remember

places. She **did not mind exploring** all the great buildings that I found.

But I also found many round holes in the ground. They looked like large wells. When I looked down one, I felt Weena's hand on my sleeve. She was trying to pull me away.

I gently shook off her weak grip. I could see only blackness in the hole. But I did feel a breath of air. I took a box of matches from my pocket. I lit one and held it over the hole. The flame was sucked downward. Air was flowing down the hole to somewhere below. But why? Who was there to breathe it?

I turned to ask Weena. She was staring at my lit match. When it went out, **her face fell**. I lit another and she clapped her hands in delight. Another surprise of the future. These people **knew nothing of fire**.

But did they know what was down below?

I looked at Weena and then pointed down the hole.

....

did not mind exploring liked

her face fell she was sad; she was disappointed

knew nothing of fire did not know what fire was

She grabbed my arm to stop me. But I was much stronger than she. I kept pointing. I demanded she answer my question.

She **gave in**. "Morlocks," she said.

I pointed at her. "Morlocks?"

She looked at me as if I were **out of my mind**. Then she pointed to herself and proudly said, "Eloi."

What she said gave me an idea. An idea that **solved many mysteries of** this strange world.

....

gave in told me the answer

out of my mind crazy

solved many mysteries of helped me understand

BEFORE YOU MOVE ON...

1. **Character** Reread page 42. How was Weena different from the other Eloi?

2. **Conclusions** Reread page 43. How did the Time Traveler know that Weena had never seen fire before?

LOOK AHEAD How does the Time Traveler meet the Morlocks? Read pages 45–48 to find out.

In this world there were two kinds of people. Masters and slaves. The masters lived above. The slaves lived below. That explained why the Eloi did not have to work. Down below, the Morlocks did all the Eloi's work for them. The Morlocks made the clothes the Eloi wore. They made the dishes and cups the Eloi ate and drank from. And everything else the Eloi needed.

I should have guessed it sooner. Even in my own time there were those who saw the world that way. Split between the rich and the poor. Between bosses and workers.

Then **another thought hit me**. Perhaps the Eloi had not stolen my Time Machine. Perhaps it was the Morlocks.

Yes, that made sense. The Morlocks were the ones who did the work. They were the ones who would be interested in machines.

But what were these Morlocks like? How could I meet them and deal with them?

The answers were waiting for me.

I kept on walking, with Weena at my side. Soon we came upon a huge building in ruins. Its

---

another thought hit me I thought of another idea

high walls cast shadows as black as night. In those shadows I saw a pale shape. Another man might have said it was a ghost. But I am a man of science. I went to find out.

I stepped into the shadows. Then I realized that Weena had **hung back**. I turned to look for her. I saw that the Eloi *did* know fear. Weena's face **was a mask of terror**. Terror of the dark.

I had no such fear. I moved straight into the darkness. I lit a match. And saw my first Morlock.

"It" is what I must call the Morlock. I could not tell if it was male or female. But I could see why the Eloi **found it so disgusting**.

The Morlock looked like a small white ape. Pale hair grew on its head and ran down its back. Its long arms hung loose by its sides. Its teeth were small and pointed. Its huge gray eyes had a red glow. They looked like they wanted to pop out of its head.

I saw all this in an instant. Then the Morlock turned and ran from my match. In its panic it ran

....

hung back not followed me

was a mask of terror looked very scared

found it so disgusting thought the Morlock was ugly

into the daylight. There it blindly ran into a tree. It shook its head. Then it dashed into the shadow of another wall.

I ran after it. But I could not catch up with it. It disappeared down a hole in the ground.

I was panting. I lit another match and looked down the hole. I saw what I had not seen before. On the side of the hole were small metal **handholds and footholds**.

This was how the Morlocks could reach the surface. This was how they could return to their underground world. And this was how I could follow them.

If I **had the nerve**.

....

handholds and footholds bars for climbing
had the nerve was brave enough

BEFORE YOU MOVE ON...

1. **Character** Why wasn't the Time Traveler scared to follow the Morlock?

2. **Foreshadowing** Writers sometimes give hints about things that will happen later. What does page 48 tell you about why Weena was scared of the holes on page 43?

LOOK AHEAD What will the Time Traveler find underground? Read pages 49–52 to find out.

The Time Traveler goes underground to find the
Morlocks. When the Morlocks see him,
he is in danger.

Chapter Six

It was hard work climbing down the hole.
The metal handholds and footholds were made for
Morlocks. And Morlocks were much smaller than I.

I looked up. I saw Weena looking down at me.
Her face was filled with horror at what I was
doing. Behind her I saw the bright blue sky. It **grew
dim** as I went deeper into the darkness.

Soon I was in total blackness. The humming of
machinery grew louder around me as I went down.

My arms and legs were aching. I stopped and lit
a match. A little below me I saw a tunnel. It went
into the side of the hole.

I reached the tunnel. I **ducked my head** to
enter it. Squeezing through was hard work. The

....

Her face was filled with horror at She looked scared about
grew dim became hard to see
ducked my head put my head down

sound of machinery grew louder and louder.

At last I came out of the tunnel. I was in a huge underground room.

I lit another match. I saw giant machines. They were going **at full blast.** Then I saw something that interested me still more: a metal table with the **leftovers of a meal**.

The leftovers were bones. Unlike the Eloi, the Morlocks still ate meat.

I bent over the bones. I wanted to find out what animals they came from. But then I saw the white creatures. Morlocks. Everywhere. Coming out of hiding among the machines. Coming toward me.

I must have scared them at first. But now **they were losing their fear.** Each time I lit a match

....

at full blast very strong

leftovers of a meal parts of food that were not eaten

they were losing their fear they were not so afraid

they froze. But each time my match went out they crept closer.

They were much smaller than I. I was sure they were much weaker. But there were so many of them. Both those I could see. And all the others I **sensed** were there.

....

sensed knew

Now I could tell they were not afraid of me. They were afraid only of my matches. Living in darkness, they could not stand bright light.

But I was afraid of them. Very afraid. Scared to the pit of my stomach. I did not know why. But I felt there was something evil about the Morlocks. Very evil.

I wanted to get out of there fast. But going through the tunnel would be slow. And slow would be dangerous. I had to buy time to escape safely.

I thought of a plan. I let my match go out. And waited.

In the darkness my heart pounded louder than the machines. Then I felt their soft little hands grabbing at me.

Instantly I lit a match. Right in the faces of the Morlocks. They were swarming over me like bugs.

They turned and fled. But not before one of them grabbed my box of matches.

BEFORE YOU MOVE ON...

1. **Inference** Reread page 49. Why do you think the Time Traveler's arm and legs were aching?

2. **Foreshadowing** Reread page 52. What gives you a hint that something bad will happen with the Morlocks?

LOOK AHEAD Will the Time Traveler escape the Morlocks? Read to page 57 to find out.

I had no time to waste. I went into the tunnel. I squeezed through as fast as I could. I tore my shirt and skinned my elbows. But I made it out the other end.

In the darkness of the hole I **groped** for the first handhold. I found it. I started upward.

I felt hands **clutching at** my legs. Pulling me down. I kicked them away.

I dragged myself up out of the hole. Never had daylight looked so beautiful. Beautiful, too, was Weena's joy. She **threw her arms around** me.

"I now know why you don't like the dark," I said to her.

But I was wrong.

I did not yet really know. Only later would I learn why Weena feared the dark. Weena and all the Eloi.

But first I found something that made my own fear go away. I found it in a building that used to be a museum.

The building was **in ruins**. No Eloi was

....

groped reached

clutching at grabbing

threw her arms around hugged

in ruins old and many parts were broken or gone

interested in a museum. But whoever built it built it well.

The glass cases were airtight. And none of them were broken. With Weena at my side, I walked among them. I saw the great inventions of the past. Inventions now forgotten by the people of the future.

Then I **spotted** the most important forgotten invention of all. A box of matches.

I smashed the glass. I struck one of the matches against the box. The match flared. I breathed a sigh of relief. Weena once again clapped her hands in delight.

As we left the museum the sun was setting. Weena pulled at my arm. She wanted to hurry. She wanted to reach the others before dark.

But it was too late for that. We had wandered too far. **Nightfall found us alone in the woods.** The rising of the moon was hours away.

Weena **clung tightly to my arm**. She was afraid of the night. Even more afraid of it than of

....

spotted saw, found

Nightfall found us alone in the woods. We were alone in the woods when it became dark.

clung tightly to my arm held my arm tightly

the shadows.

Soon I knew why. I heard Morlock feet running all around us. And grunting Morlock voices. I felt Weena let go of my arm.

In my hand I carried a metal bar. I had used it to smash the glass case in the museum. But I realized it was useless now. There were too many Morlocks around. Far too many to fight in the dark.

But I did have a weapon that would work. Swiftly I struck a match.

I saw Weena lying at my feet. She **had fainted dead away**.

And in a circle around us Morlocks were closing in. Wave upon wave of them. **Hideous and hungering.** I could not **hold them off** for long. Only for as long as my matches lasted.

I wish I could boast how smart my next move was. But it was very simple. A cave man would have done the same thing millions of years ago.

I built a fire.

I started with dry twigs. Then I added thick

....

had fainted dead away became so afraid that she fell
Hideous and hungering. The Morlocks looked scary and hungry.
hold them off make them stay away

branches I snapped off of trees. I soon had a fire burning brightly. Its light protected us from the Morlocks. It was like a **fortress** wall.

I lay Weena beside the fire. I hoped **its warmth would waken her**. But it did not. And the warmth did the opposite to me.

I had traveled hundreds of thousands of years through time. I had been exploring the future for days **with no letup**. I was **bone tired**. I fell asleep.

....

fortress very strong

its warmth would waken her she would wake up when she felt the warm fire

with no letup without being able to rest

bone tired very tired

I woke to darkness. With so many little hands clutching my arms and legs. And so many little teeth nipping at my skin.

BEFORE YOU MOVE ON...

1. **Foreshadowing** Find the sentence on page 53 that tells that the Time Traveler will learn something important about the darkness.

2. **Character's Point of View** Why did the Time Traveler think that matches were the most important invention of all?

LOOK AHEAD Read to page 63 to find out what miracle saves the Time Traveler.

The Time Traveler realizes the Morlocks are taking care of the Eloi so that they can eat them. The Time Traveler tries again to get his machine back.

Chapter Seven

I felt for my box of matches. It was gone. The Morlocks were smart. **Cunning** at least. They had figured out that my matches meant danger. Again they had stolen them from me.

I still had my metal bar. I hit out with it in the dark. I felt it **make contact**. I heard cries of pain.

But there were too many hands attacking me. Too many teeth. Soon my arm began to tire.

It seemed only a miracle could save me. And something close to a miracle did.

There was a burst of light. And the attacking Morlocks **melted away**.

....

Cunning Clever
make contact hit them
melted away went away quietly

For a moment I could not see. I **was blinded by the glare**. Then I saw that the light came from a nearby bush. The bush **had burst into flame**.

A spark from my dying fire must have started it burning. The sun in this world of the future was much stronger. The bush was still very dry from the hot day before. Flames leaped up from it. A tree beside it began to burn.

The Morlocks were caught in the wildfire. They were blinded by its light. **In their terror** they ran into each other. Into trees. Even into the flames.

A few died. The rest found their holes and escaped. I relaxed. The fire was burning itself out. But **dawn was breaking**. I was safe.

Then I stopped thinking of myself. I remembered Weena. She was gone.

The Morlocks must have taken her. But why? I knew why they had come after me. They saw me as an enemy. I had **invaded** their underground home. But why Weena? She would not hurt a fly.

....

was blinded by the glare could not see because of the light
had burst into flame started to burn
In their terror Because they were afraid
dawn was breaking the sun was coming up
invaded gone in; entered like an enemy into

Weena must have known the answer. I remembered her fear of the dark. But it was not the dark she feared. It was the Morlocks.

Then I remembered something else. The bones on the Morlocks' table. Where had they come from in a world without animals?

And I knew the secret of the future. The horrifying secret.

I had been right about one thing. The human race had been split into two races. The Eloi and the Morlocks. But I had been very wrong about everything else.

Once perhaps the Eloi had been the masters. The Morlocks had been the slaves. But that time was over.

The Eloi must have grown too **soft** and lazy to feed the Morlocks. And the Morlocks had found their own food. Perhaps out of hunger. Or perhaps out of hate.

The Morlocks still made clothes and other things for the Eloi. But not like slaves working for masters. Instead they were like farmers taking care of **livestock**. Livestock that they wanted healthy

....

soft weak

livestock animals that will be killed and eaten

and **tender**.

That was what the Eloi were. No more than cattle. Cattle kept alive for only one reason. So that in the dark the Morlocks could come for them. So that the Morlocks' dinner plates would always be full.

I smiled sadly. Now I knew why the Eloi had no graveyards. Why there were no old or sick among them. Once I had thought **they had conquered death**. What a cruel joke. Death, the most terrible kind of death, ruled over them.

....

tender easy to eat
they had conquered death none of them ever died

BEFORE YOU MOVE ON...

1. **Cause and Effect** Reread page 60. A fire drove the Morlocks away. Why did it start?

2. **Summarize** Reread pages 62–63. What did the Time Traveler say about the Morlocks and the Eloi?

LOOK AHEAD The Time Traveler really wants to get home now. Read pages 64–67 to find out what he does next.

In the east I saw the dawn. I shivered. I could not stand to stay in this world any longer. I could not stand seeing the Eloi again. Not now that I knew what they were. And what would happen to them.

Besides, now the Morlocks were after me, too. They would not **rest until they got their hands on me**. Their teeth into me. Sooner or later I would **let down my guard**. And they would get what they wanted.

I had to get out. I had to **get my hands on** the Time Machine.

It was still locked in the base of the White Sphinx. I weighed the metal bar in my hand. Perhaps it could break open the bronze door.

I hoped so. I had no other tools. Unless I found a use for a few matches still in my pocket. They must have **slipped** out of the box before it was stolen.

The day was hot and bright by the time I reached the White Sphinx. Its worn face seemed to smile down at me.

....

rest until they got their hands on me stop chasing me
let down my guard forget to watch for the Morlocks
get my hands on hurry and find
slipped fallen

"Now I know why you're smiling," I said to it. "I know your horrible joke. I know the answer to the **riddle** of the future."

Then I lifted my bar to smash the bronze door. But before I could, I heard a sound. A **whirring noise**. The door slowly slid open.

There was my Time Machine. Right inside the hollow base.

....

riddle question
whirring noise low sound

It looked like it was **in good shape**. In fact, it was in much better shape than I expected. Dents had been smoothed out. Every inch was oiled and polished. The Morlocks took good care of machines.

I let my bar drop. Quickly I checked my pockets. I made sure I still had the two ivory levers. The levers that worked the Time Machine.

Then I stepped inside the base. I had to reach the machine. Even though I guessed what was going to happen. And it did.

The door **swiftly** slid shut. I was trapped in the dark.

The Morlocks must have been proud of their trap. I heard chuckling grunts as they closed in on me. I smelled their disgusting bodies.

But they were not dealing with a childlike Eloi. I **had seen through** their trick. I was prepared.

Already I had a match in my hand. When **it flared**, the Morlocks would retreat. I would be able to put the levers back into the Time Machine. I would give a pull.

....

in good shape still working
swiftly quickly
had seen through was not fooled by
it flared they saw the fire

And I would be out of this trap. Out of this nightmare future world. I would be **heading back** to my own world. My own time.

Smiling, I struck the match against the inside of the door.

Nothing happened.

I tried again.

Still nothing.

I had forgotten one detail. One **deadly detail**.

The matches were the wrong kind. **They lit only when struck against** the side of their box.

They **were useless** here. And the Morlocks' hands were already grabbing at me in the dark.

....

heading back going, returning

deadly detail thing that could cause my death

They lit only when struck against I could light the match only if I used

were useless would not make fire

BEFORE YOU MOVE ON...

1. **Inference** The Time Traveler went back to the Sphinx for his machine. Why did he want to leave so badly?

2. **Details** Reread pages 66–67. How did the Time Traveler plan to escape from the Morlocks?

LOOK AHEAD Read pages 68–72 to find out if the Time Traveler escaped.

The Time Traveler starts the Time Machine and goes far into the future. When he comes back, he has many new ideas.

Chapter Eight

I did not try to fight off those hands. There were too many of them. **I did not have the time to spare.** My only chance was to make my move fast. Before any more of the Morlocks grabbed me.

I **felt my way to** the seat of the Time Machine. Dragging Morlocks with me, I sat down in it. I found the openings for the levers. I shoved one into place. Then the other.

By now the Morlocks were almost pulling me from my seat. Their hands were cold and damp. Their warm breath **stank**.

....

I did not have the time to spare. I had to move quickly to return to the Time Machine.

felt my way to reached for

stank smelled bad

I put all my strength into a sweep of my arm. A savage sweep that sent the Morlocks flying. Then I pulled down on the time-travel lever as hard as I could.

For a moment I thought I would die. The machine was not made to be started that way.

But it worked! That was the important thing. I looked at the dial. The Morlocks were a million years behind me.

True, I had pulled the lever the wrong way. I was going into the future, not the past. But I did not mind. I would take another look at **things to come**.

....

I put all my strength into a sweep of my arm. I swung my arm as hard as I could.

things to come the future

Then I would head back.

I **brought the machine to a stop**. I found myself on an empty beach. It was on the edge of a

---

brought the machine to a stop stopped the machine

smooth, dead sea. The only signs of life were a few crawling crabs. The sun was a huge red ball. The air was as hot as an oven.

The earth was very close to the sun now. Soon it would burn up. I wiped sweat from my **brow**. I was lucky to stop when I did. Before I reached the end of the world. And my own end as well.

I pushed the lever up to **send me** back through time. Back to the year 1895. Back to the evening of September 22.

This time I watched the dials closely. When I reached 1900, I slowed the machine. I passed into 1895. I slowed it still more. Then I brought it to a sharp stop.

....

brow forehead

send me make me travel

BEFORE YOU MOVE ON...

1. **Sequence** Tell the events that happened before the Time Traveler finally reached home.

2. **Character** Reread page 70. What do you know about the Time Traveler that helps you understand why he didn't mind going farther into the future?

LOOK AHEAD Read pages 73–77 to see if the Time Traveler's friends are waiting for him.

I was back in my laboratory. I got out of the machine. I looked in a mirror. My face was **unshaven**. My clothes were dusty and torn. No matter. My friends would understand.

I entered the dining room. They were just finishing dinner.

"I hope you enjoyed the meal," I said. "I told my housekeeper to do her very best."

"It was fine," the writer said. He smacked his lips.

"Delicious," said the politician. He was finishing the last crumbs of his cake.

"You'll have to tell quite a tasty tale to **top it**." The psychologist was smiling as he spoke.

"I will let you **be the judge of** that," I said. I sat down at the head of the table. And I told them my story.

When I finished, my friends looked at one another.

The doctor spoke for all of them.

"It's a wonderful story," he said. "But do you have proof?"

....

unshaven hairy
top it be better than the meal
be the judge of decide

"I can give you only my **word of honor**," I said. Their faces fell. Then I added, "Oh, yes, and this."

I pulled from my pocket a handful of flowers. The flowers that Weena gave me after I saved her life. I handed them to the doctor. I knew his hobby was the study of flowers.

He looked at them closely. At last he spoke. "I've never seen flowers like these," he admitted.

....

word of honor promise

"Nor will you. Unless you travel in my Time Machine," I told him. "They are proof of my story."

I looked at the flowers sadly. I thought of Weena. I could almost see her again.

"They are proof of something else, too," I said. "Proof that people of the future still could feel gratitude. They still could feel love."

"Too bad your story has such an unhappy ending," said the writer. He shook his head. "It's a pity about Weena. And **even more of a pity** about the human race."

"Perhaps I can **come up with a different ending**," I said. "I'll see what I can do. Please come to dinner next week. I'll have another story for you."

I told them nothing more. Only now will I write down what I plan to do. Then I will get in the Time Machine again.

I will return to 802,701 A.D. I will arrive among the Eloi once more. But this time I will bring them a gift. The gift of knowledge.

....

even more of a pity sadder

come up with a different ending do something that will change the end of the story

I will teach them what **earliest man** had to learn. I will teach them how to use fire.

Perhaps that will let them **drive off** the Morlocks. Perhaps that will make them brave. Perhaps they will start to stand on their own feet. Perhaps they will grow to become *human*.

Perhaps.

All I can do is give them the chance. All I can do is **put their fate into their own hands**.

All I can do as I **set out** in my Time Machine is hope.

....

earliest man people who lived very long ago

drive off fight

put their fate into their own hands help them control what happens to them

set out leave

BEFORE YOU MOVE ON...

1. **Plot** Where were the Time Traveler's friends when he came back to his own time? Did they seem to believe his story?

2. **Character's Motive** Reread pages 76–77. Why did the Time Traveler say he would go to the year 802,701 A.D. again?

LOOK AHEAD A new person tells the end of the story. Read page 78 to find out who.

A Final Note

This is not the Time Traveler who is writing now. This is his friend, the writer.

His other friends and I found the story you have just read. It was on the dining-room table when we arrived the next week.

Since then we have been waiting for the Time Traveler. Waiting for him to **give us the final chapter**.

But the Time Traveler set off on his journey three years ago.

And he has not yet returned.

The End?

....

give us the final chapter tell us what happened to him

> **BEFORE YOU MOVE ON...**
>
> 1. **Narrator** Who told the last part of the story? Why?
>
> 2. **Inference** How do you know the friends believed the Time Traveler went to the future?